Patience
Teri Dou

Patience of the Heart

Teri Dourmashkin

Published by Teri Dourmashkin, 2024.

This is a work of fiction. Similarities to real people, places, or events are entirely coincidental.

PATIENCE OF THE HEART

First edition. October 30, 2024.

Copyright © 2024 Teri Dourmashkin.

ISBN: 979-8224612505

Written by Teri Dourmashkin.

Table of Contents

Chapter 1: First Glimpse 1
Chapter 2: Opening Up 6
Chapter 3: Seeds of Doubt 11
Chapter 4: A Glimmer of Hope 17
Chapter 5: Emotional Distance 22
Chapter 6: Crisis Point 27
Chapter 7: Dreams of What Could Be 32
Chapter 8: The First Attempt 37
Chapter 9: Holding On Through the Storm 42
Chapter 10: Breaking Free 47
Chapter 11: The Long-Awaited Meeting 52
Chapter 12: A New Beginning 57

To those who have loved, lost, and found the courage to begin again. To my readers, thank you for joining me on this journey of hope and renewal. To my friends and family, your unwavering support has been the light that guided me here.

To my dear friends Mina, Court, Dave, and Bill—your presence in my life has been a source of joy and strength. And to my friend Blue, for your invaluable friendship and guidance in helping me craft my poetry and this story, I am forever grateful.

May this story remind us all that love, patience, and resilience create miracles every day.

Chapter 1: First Glimpse

Leila sat hunched over her laptop, her fingers resting idly on the keyboard as the dim glow of the screen reflected off her tired eyes. The room around her was still, the only sounds the occasional hum of the air conditioner and the quiet rustle of the leaves brushing against the window. The day had felt long, the kind that weighed heavily on her mind and body, leaving her searching for some kind of release—something beyond the usual distraction of social media or the background noise of television.

She clicked mindlessly through various websites, her mind half-distracted, until a link caught her eye: Hearts Unveiled Poetry Forum. Her brow furrowed slightly, curiosity piqued. Leila wasn't usually one for forums, especially not those filled with strangers sharing pieces of their lives, but something in the title pulled her in. She clicked on the link, and the page that loaded was a simple one—nothing flashy, just poems and conversations between people from all over the world.

Her eyes skimmed the first few entries, each one a little window into someone else's soul. Some poems were lighthearted, some were filled with raw pain, but each was an offering, a connection. There was a certain openness in the way the words spilled across the page, as if the distance of the internet gave people the freedom to say what they couldn't in their everyday lives. Leila's gaze settled on one poem in particular:

"Faith is a seed in the darkest of times,
Watered by hope, it rises to climb."

She read it again, slower this time, letting the simplicity of the lines sink in. It wasn't overly elaborate, but there was something honest about it—something that felt like it had been written not to impress, but to offer comfort. Leila couldn't quite explain why, but those words seemed to echo something inside her, something she hadn't been able to put into words herself.

She clicked on the username: DavidEvergreen. Curious, she began scrolling through his posts. There were more poems, each one imbued with the same quiet strength, a sense of optimism that felt genuine, not forced. It was the kind of hope that didn't shout or demand to be heard—it whispered, gently reminding you that it was there, even in the darkest moments.

For a moment, Leila hesitated. She wasn't usually one to comment on things like this—especially not to strangers. But something about his words made her want to reach out. She started typing, her fingers moving slowly across the keyboard, feeling a little vulnerable.

LeilaWrites: This is beautiful. It's exactly what I needed to read tonight. Thank you for sharing.

Her finger hovered over the send button for a moment before she pressed it. Immediately, she felt a small knot of anxiety twist in her stomach. Why did she feel so exposed? It was just a comment, after all. But something about this small exchange felt more meaningful than her usual online interactions.

Minutes passed, and she tried to distract herself by scrolling through other poems. But her attention kept wandering back to

David's words, and the fact that she had opened herself up, even just a little. The notification icon blinked at the top of the page, and her heart jumped slightly as she clicked it.

DavidEvergreen: I'm glad it resonated with you, Leila. Poetry is like that sometimes, reaching the right people at the right time.

A small smile tugged at her lips. There was a warmth in his response, a sincerity that felt real, even across the digital space. She read the reply again, feeling oddly comforted by the fact that someone out there understood what she was feeling—even if it was just a brief moment of connection.

As she scrolled down the page, she noticed other users had commented on the poem too.

PoetryLover88: Wow, this one hit deep. We all need that reminder to keep hoping.

StarryNights: I agree. David's poems always seem to have that touch of hope. It's what keeps me coming back to this forum.

The sense of community on the forum was palpable. It was as if these people, scattered across the world, were all reaching out to each other in their own way, sharing their thoughts and emotions in a space where they felt seen. Leila found herself scrolling through the thread, not just reading David's poems but diving into the conversations that followed. Each comment, each response, was like a little thread weaving a tapestry of shared human experience.

But despite the dozens of posts she skimmed through, she kept returning to David's words. There was something about him—something grounding, something that made her feel like she wasn't so alone in her own struggles. She wasn't sure why, but she felt drawn to him, his quiet strength a comfort she didn't realize she'd been searching for.

Later that evening, as the forum grew quieter, Leila sat with her hands resting on the keyboard, debating whether to send him a private message. She wasn't the type to reach out to strangers, especially not like this, but something about tonight felt different. Maybe it was the way his words had resonated with her. Maybe it was the anonymity of the forum that made it feel safer than her everyday life. Whatever the reason, she found herself typing.

LeilaWrites: Hi, David. I hope you don't mind me messaging you directly. Your poetry really spoke to me today. Do you write often?

She hit send before she could second-guess herself, her heart beating just a little faster. The vulnerability in reaching out was unsettling, but it also felt... right.

The response didn't take long.

DavidEvergreen: Hey, Leila. Thanks for reaching out. I do write often, though usually it's just for myself. The forum's been a great place to share when I feel like someone might connect with what I'm feeling. What about you? Are you a writer, too?

Leila stared at the screen for a moment, surprised by how easy it was to talk to him. She smiled to herself, then started typing again.

LeilaWrites: I write sometimes, but nothing like you. I mostly journal, just trying to make sense of things. Life's been a bit of a mess lately, and writing helps clear my head.

She hit send, her heart still racing slightly. Why was she telling him this? She barely knew him. But there was something about the anonymity of the forum that made it easier to be honest, to share the parts of herself she usually kept hidden.

A few minutes later, his reply popped up.

DavidEvergreen: That's the beauty of writing, I think. It doesn't have to be perfect or for anyone else. It's just about finding clarity in the chaos. I'm glad you've found that outlet. If you ever want to share anything, I'd love to read it.

Leila leaned back in her chair, a soft smile tugging at her lips. There was something about this—this connection, this feeling of being understood by someone she didn't even know—that felt strangely comforting. Maybe there was more to this online world than she had thought.

The conversation between them flowed easily after that, moving between poetry and personal stories, their words weaving a connection that felt natural, unforced. The hours slipped by, and before Leila knew it, the sun was beginning to rise, casting soft golden light across her living room. As they exchanged their final messages for the night, Leila felt something shift inside her. It was subtle, but it was there—a spark of hope she hadn't felt in a long time.

As she closed her laptop and crawled into bed, her thoughts drifted back to David's words. There was something about him—something genuine, something that made her want to keep talking, keep exploring. But there was also a voice in the back of her mind, reminding her that this was just the internet. How real could it possibly be?

Still, as she drifted off to sleep, her thoughts returned to the words that had started it all:

"Faith is a seed in the darkest of times,
Watered by hope, it rises to climb."

Chapter 2: Opening Up

Leila sat at her desk, fingers resting on the smooth surface of her laptop, the gentle hum of the machine filling the otherwise quiet room. A cup of tea sat untouched beside her, its warmth slowly fading as she stared at the familiar notification icon on the poetry forum. She had messaged David again last night, and now there it was—his reply waiting for her.

A week had passed since their first exchange, and each day since had brought more words between them. It was strange, the way he seemed to have slipped into her daily routine without her even realizing it. What had started as a simple comment on a poem had turned into a series of conversations that stretched into the late hours of the night, sometimes well past when she would normally have fallen asleep.

There was something about David that drew her in—his words, his kindness, and the quiet strength that seemed to seep through every message. She had never spoken to anyone like this before, certainly not someone she had never met. But with David, it felt... easy.

Leila clicked on the notification, her heart giving a small flutter as she opened the message.

DavidEvergreen: Morning, Leila. I hope you're doing well. I was thinking about what you said last night about feeling stuck. I know that feeling all too well. I don't talk about it much, but my own marriage has been... well, let's just say it's not what I thought it would be. We've grown apart, and I don't know how to fix that. I guess that's why I turn to poetry—it's the only thing that still makes sense to me sometimes. Anyway, I don't want to unload too much. Just wanted you to know that I get it.

Leila stared at the message, a tight knot forming in her chest. She hadn't expected him to open up like that. They had shared personal thoughts before, but this was different. This was real pain, the kind she recognized all too well.

Her hands hovered over the keys, unsure of how to respond. She felt a strange mix of emotions—gratitude that he trusted her enough to share this, and sadness that he was going through something so similar to her own struggles. Finally, she began to type.

LeilaWrites: David, I'm sorry to hear that. It sounds really tough, and I can understand how poetry would help. Writing has always been an outlet for me too, especially when things get hard. I haven't talked much about it, but I've been in the same place for a while now. My marriage... well, it's been a lot of pretending. I don't know how to fix it either. Sometimes I wonder if it's even worth fixing.

She paused, reading her words over before hitting send. Her fingers trembled slightly as she let out a breath she didn't realize she was holding. It wasn't like her to be this open, especially not with someone she barely knew. But with David, it felt different. It felt safe.

Moments later, his reply came through.

DavidEvergreen: I'm really sorry you're dealing with that, Leila. I know it's hard. It's like you're stuck in this place where you don't recognize yourself anymore, but you also don't know how to change things. I don't have the answers, but I'm here if you ever need to talk. Sometimes, just having someone to listen can make all the difference.

His words hit her harder than she expected. It wasn't just what he said—it was how he said it. There was no judgment, no empty advice, just the quiet reassurance that he was there, listening. Leila realized that she hadn't had that in a long time.

LeilaWrites: Thank you. It means a lot to know I'm not alone in this. And I think you're right—sometimes it's enough just to have someone to talk to. I guess that's why I've been writing more lately. It helps me sort through the mess in my head.

They continued messaging for the next hour, their conversation flowing effortlessly between serious topics and lighter ones. They talked about the books they were reading, the songs that got stuck in their heads, and the little moments of joy they found in their everyday lives. But beneath it all, there was an unspoken understanding—a shared pain that connected them in a way they hadn't expected.

As the days passed, Leila found herself looking forward to their conversations more and more. Each message from David felt like a lifeline, pulling her out of the darkness that had settled over her life. She hadn't realized just how isolated she had been until now, when she finally had someone to share her thoughts with—someone who understood, without needing to explain.

One evening, after a particularly difficult day, Leila sat down at her desk and opened her laptop, feeling the weight of the day pressing down on her. She hadn't heard from David yet, but she found herself drawn to the poetry forum nonetheless. She scrolled through the latest posts, her eyes scanning the words of strangers, but nothing seemed to catch her attention.

And then she saw it—David's latest poem, posted just minutes earlier.

"In silence, we sit beneath the weight of unsaid words,
But in the quiet, I hear you."

Leila read the poem again, and again, feeling the familiar warmth of his words wrap around her like a blanket. It was simple, like all of David's poems, but there was something in it that spoke directly to her. It was as if he had written it for her, as if he had known exactly what she needed to hear in that moment.

Without thinking, she opened the message box and started typing.

LeilaWrites: Your poem… it's beautiful, David. It's exactly how I feel right now. Sometimes I don't even know what to say, but it's like you get it anyway.

She hit send, her heart pounding in her chest. She hadn't meant to be so forward, but the words had spilled out before she could stop them. She stared at the screen, waiting for his response, feeling more vulnerable than she had in a long time.

His reply came through quickly.

DavidEvergreen: I'm glad it spoke to you. I wrote it because I was thinking about our conversations. I know things have been hard for both of us, but even when we don't have all the answers, just knowing you're there makes a difference. I hope you know that.

Leila felt her breath catch in her throat. She hadn't expected him to say that, hadn't realized just how much their conversations meant to him too. For the first time in a long while, she felt a glimmer of something she hadn't allowed herself to feel in years—hope.

But with that hope came fear. What were they doing? She barely knew him, and yet here they were, sharing their most personal thoughts, leaning on each other in a way that felt more intimate than anything she had experienced in her own marriage. It scared her, the depth of the connection she was starting to feel.

But it was also undeniable.

Leila closed her laptop, her mind swirling with thoughts and emotions she wasn't ready to confront. She wasn't sure what was happening between her and David, or where this was headed, but she knew one thing for certain—she didn't want it to stop.

Chapter 3: Seeds of Doubt

Leila hadn't realized just how much her conversations with David had become a part of her life until she started to pull back. It wasn't intentional at first—just a few messages left unanswered, a day or two without checking the forum. But as the days passed, the quiet space between them began to grow, filled with an anxious, gnawing uncertainty she couldn't shake. It was as if by pulling back, she was both protecting herself and risking something precious, something she couldn't quite understand yet.

She leaned back in her chair, eyes unfocused on the screen in front of her. The cursor blinked in the message box where she had started typing and stopped. Half-formed words lingered there, a hesitant apology she wasn't sure how to finish. The truth was, she didn't know what to say. She wasn't even sure what she was feeling, a muddle of emotions tangled together, making her doubt her own heart. She wasn't used to feeling this uncertain, especially not over someone she had never even met.

Leila's thoughts drifted, her mind filled with snippets of conversations with David. His words had a way of sticking with her, comforting yet unsettling in their sincerity. They made her feel seen, understood in a way she hadn't felt in years. But wasn't that part of the problem? How could she let herself care so much for someone who existed only through words on a screen? And yet, the thought of losing that connection filled her with an ache she couldn't quite explain, a longing she didn't know she was capable of feeling.

Her eyes dropped to her hands, resting in her lap. She clenched and unclenched her fingers, feeling the tension that had settled there. Her chronic pain had been worsening lately, each ache and throb a reminder of the weight she carried, both physically and emotionally. She rubbed her temples, closing her eyes against the familiar sting that had become a near-constant companion in her life. Sometimes, it felt like the pain was a wall between her and the world, separating her from the things she wanted, the things that made her feel alive.

And then there was David—a stranger who, against all odds, had managed to slip past that wall, his words reaching her in places she had almost forgotten existed. But that was the problem, wasn't it? She was starting to need him, starting to rely on him in a way that scared her. She had built her life around control, around keeping her emotions in check, and now here she was, letting a stranger disrupt it all with nothing more than a few lines of poetry.

The message box blinked, a new message from him lighting up her screen. She stared at it, a flicker of guilt twisting in her chest. She hadn't replied to his last message, and now here he was again, reaching out, patient as ever.

David's words appeared on the screen:

DavidEvergreen: *Hey, Leila. I just wanted to check in. I hope you're doing okay. No pressure to reply, just... wanted you to know I'm here if you need anything.*

Her heart gave a small, painful squeeze. There he was again—reassuring, understanding, never asking for more than she was willing to give. She hated how much she needed that, how much she had come to rely on his presence, his steady faith. It scared her, the way he had become such a central part of her life, even from miles away. It was like he had found a way into the quiet spaces of her mind, places she didn't let anyone else go.

Leila let out a shaky breath and closed her laptop, unable to bring herself to respond. She needed space to think, to breathe, to figure out what was happening to her. She couldn't keep leaning on him like this—it wasn't fair, to him or to herself. But the thought of pushing him away felt like tearing out a part of her heart, a wound she wasn't sure she could bear.

Days passed in a blur, filled with the usual rhythm of her life, but something felt off. She went through the motions—work, chores, evenings filled with quiet solitude—but the emptiness had grown sharper, deeper, like a hollow ache that refused to leave. She missed their conversations, missed the way David's words had filled her mind with warmth and hope, even on the darkest days. Without him, the silence felt heavier, more oppressive, pressing down on her with a weight she couldn't shake.

One evening, after a particularly rough day, Leila found herself lying on her bed, staring at the ceiling, feeling the weight of her loneliness pressing down on her. Her phone buzzed on the nightstand, a small, persistent reminder of the world outside. She reached over, expecting another notification, but instead saw a text from an unfamiliar number.

It's David. I hope this isn't too forward, but I wanted to share something with you. It's been a while, and I just... I miss our conversations.

Her heart skipped a beat. She hadn't realized just how much she'd missed hearing from him until now, his name lighting up her screen like a beacon in the dark. Attached to the message was a photo—a handwritten poem, his familiar scrawl filling the page.

"Patience is the seed we plant in the dark,
Hidden beneath the weight of the earth.
It waits, quietly, until the time is right,
Knowing that in stillness, it will find its worth."

Leila read the words slowly, feeling the weight of each line settle over her. She read them again, her fingers tracing the letters on the screen as if trying to touch a part of him through the distance. It was a reminder of everything he had been trying to tell her—that love, real love, wasn't something to be rushed. It needed time to grow, time to breathe, to take root in the spaces between their conversations and the silences that filled their lives.

She stared at the poem, her eyes blurring slightly as a tear slipped down her cheek. David understood, in a way she hadn't expected. He wasn't pushing her, wasn't demanding an explanation. He was just... there, waiting, letting her find her own way back to him. It was a gift, this patience of his, a quiet strength she hadn't realized she needed until now.

With a shaky hand, she typed out a reply.

LeilaWrites: *Thank you, David. I needed that. I'm sorry for pulling away. It's just... hard. Sometimes I don't know what I'm doing, or where this is going, and it scares me. But your words... they remind me that maybe it's okay not to have all the answers.*

She hit send before she could overthink it, her heart pounding in her chest as she waited for his response. It felt strange, sharing her fears like this, but also freeing. In that moment, she felt lighter, as if a weight had lifted from her shoulders, leaving her breathless and unsure, yet somehow at peace.

A moment later, his reply came through.

DavidEvergreen: *Leila, you don't have to apologize. I get it. This whole thing... it's new for me too. But I believe that some things are worth waiting for, even if they don't make sense right away. I'm here, as long as you need me to be.*

His words settled over her, a warm reassurance that filled the empty spaces in her heart. For the first time in days, she felt a flicker of hope—a quiet, steady belief that maybe, just maybe, they could figure this out together. She hadn't expected him to be so patient, so understanding, and the depth of his kindness left her feeling both grateful and vulnerable.

They continued their conversation, slipping back into the familiar rhythm of shared stories and gentle encouragements. But something had shifted between them. Leila's fear was still there, a constant whisper in the back of her mind, but it was softened by David's presence, his steady faith that they would find their way through the uncertainty.

As the evening wore on, they exchanged poems and pieces of themselves, sharing their doubts and dreams in a way that felt real, raw. It wasn't perfect, but it was honest, and that was enough. They were both flawed, both broken in their own ways, yet somehow they had found a sense of peace in each other's company.

Leila leaned back, closing her eyes as David's words lingered in her mind. She didn't know what the future held, didn't know if they would ever find a way to bridge the distance between them. But for now, she was content to let things unfold, to give their connection the space it needed to grow.

As she drifted off to sleep, she thought of his poem, the words etched in her mind like a quiet promise, a reminder of the patience they would need as they navigated the uncertain path ahead:

"Patience is the seed we plant in the dark...
Knowing that in stillness, it will find its worth."

Chapter 4: A Glimmer of Hope

Leila sat by her window, watching the early morning light creep into her living room, casting soft shadows across the furniture. She held her phone in her hand, rereading David's last message, her fingers lingering over the screen as if his words could somehow bridge the miles that separated them. She had been feeling lost, her mind clouded with doubt, but his message had been like a hand reaching out to her, steadying her when she'd felt on the verge of slipping.

It was simple, really, the way he seemed to know what she needed, even when she couldn't find the words herself. In his message, he had written: "I believe in us, Leila. I don't know where this will lead, but I know that something brought us together, and I trust that. Take your time. I'll be here."

She read those words over and over, letting their meaning sink in. His faith in them was unshakable, a quiet certainty that had become her anchor in the swirling storm of her own insecurities. She hadn't known that she could feel this way—that someone's words, their presence, could feel like a lifeline. It was as if David saw something in her that she had never dared to see in herself, a possibility, a glimmer of happiness that felt both frightening and exhilarating.

Setting her phone down, she wrapped herself in a blanket and sat on the couch, her thoughts drifting back to the moments they'd shared over the past few weeks. There was a rhythm to their conversations now, a familiarity that felt as natural as breathing. Each message from him was a reminder that, somewhere out there, there was someone who cared, someone who was waiting for her, believing in her.

Leila found herself smiling, a small, tentative smile that felt foreign yet welcome. For the first time in a long time, the weight on her chest seemed lighter, as if David's belief in them had somehow transferred to her, nudging her toward the idea that maybe, just maybe, happiness wasn't as far out of reach as she'd once thought.

The quiet buzz of her phone pulled her back to the present, and her heart skipped as she saw his name on the screen. She opened the message, her smile widening as she read his words.

DavidEvergreen: I wrote something for you this morning. I hope it brings a little light to your day.

Below his message was a new poem, each line carefully written, a piece of his heart offered up to her.

"*When the darkness presses close, and the world feels far too wide,*

Hold on to the thread of hope, and know I'm by your side."

"*Though miles may lie between us, and doubt may cloud the way,*

Believe that love can find us, even through the gray."

Leila read the poem, her fingers grazing the screen as if she could feel the warmth of his words. It was so simple, so gentle, yet it held a strength that took her breath away. She felt tears prick at the corners of her eyes, and for once, she didn't try to push them away. She let herself feel the quiet joy that his words brought, let herself hold on to that glimmer of hope he had offered her.

She typed out a reply, her fingers moving slowly as she chose each word carefully.

LeilaWrites: *David, thank you. Your words... they mean more to me than I can say. It's been so long since I've felt this way, like there's something worth holding on to. You make me feel like happiness is possible again.*

She paused, staring at her message before hitting send. It was an admission she hadn't intended to make, a vulnerability she hadn't planned to share. But with David, it felt safe, like she could let down the walls she had built so carefully around her heart.

His response came almost immediately, and she could almost picture him on the other side, reading her words with that quiet smile she had come to imagine.

DavidEvergreen: *Leila, you deserve happiness. Don't let anyone, especially yourself, tell you otherwise. I'll be here, however long it takes. We'll find our way through this together.*

Leila took a deep breath, feeling the warmth of his words settle over her. She closed her eyes, letting herself believe, just for a moment, that happiness was within her reach. The fear was still there, a shadow lurking in the background, but it was softer now, tempered by the light he had brought into her life.

Days passed in a gentle rhythm, their conversations weaving a tapestry of shared dreams and quiet hopes. They spoke of the future in tentative whispers, neither daring to voice the full extent of their wishes, yet both feeling the pull of something more, something real.

One evening, as they exchanged messages, David surprised her with another poem, this one filled with a quiet, unwavering faith that seemed to reach across the distance between them.

"In the quiet moments between, I feel you close, a breath, a thought.

Though we are worlds apart, our hearts are not."

Leila read the poem, her heart swelling with a mix of joy and fear. She wanted to believe in this, wanted to trust that the universe had brought them together for a reason. But a part of her still held back, a small, fearful part that whispered doubts into her mind, reminding her of the pain she had endured, the times she had dared to hope only to be disappointed.

Yet David's words, his steady presence, were like a beacon, guiding her through the fog of her own insecurities. She could feel herself beginning to open up, beginning to let go of the fears that had held her captive for so long. She didn't know where this path would lead, didn't know if they would ever bridge the distance between them, but for the first time, she was willing to try.

One night, as they shared their hopes and fears, David sent her a simple message, a reminder of everything he had come to mean to her.

DavidEvergreen: *Leila, no matter where life takes us, I'm grateful for this—grateful for you. Remember that.*

She sat in the quiet of her room, his words a soft echo in her mind. She wanted to reply, to tell him how much he had come to mean to her, but the words felt inadequate, too small to hold the weight of her feelings. Instead, she closed her eyes, letting herself imagine him there beside her, his presence a comforting warmth that soothed the ache of loneliness.

As she drifted off to sleep, she held on to that small, growing hope, a quiet, tentative belief that maybe, just maybe, happiness was within her reach. It was a fragile thing, like the first green shoots of spring, but it was there, a promise of something more.

Chapter 5: Emotional Distance

Leila sat alone in her quiet apartment, the world outside obscured by the evening's darkening sky. The soft glow of her laptop screen was the only light in the room, casting her face in a gentle haze as she reread David's last message. She felt her chest tighten, an inexplicable pang of sadness mingling with the quiet joy his words brought. It was the same tug-of-war that had been simmering beneath the surface, a clash between her longing for something real and the doubts that refused to let go.

David's messages had always been a source of comfort, a steady rhythm in the unpredictable pulse of her life. But tonight, as she read his words, that comfort felt distant, shadowed by a familiar sense of fear she couldn't ignore.

"Sometimes, I wonder if this is all in my head," she whispered to herself, the words filling the silence. She couldn't tell him that, couldn't let him see the cracks forming beneath the surface. David had always been so patient, so sure, but she was starting to wonder if her heart was strong enough to keep believing. What if this was nothing more than a beautiful illusion, a fantasy crafted in the quiet spaces of her loneliness?

The sound of her phone chimed softly beside her, breaking the quiet. She glanced down to see his name, a tiny notification that felt like a lifeline and a reminder of the emotional distance she had started to create between them.

DavidEvergreen: Leila, I hope today was kind to you. I wanted to share something I wrote this morning. I hope it speaks to you.

Her heart softened as she opened the message, her doubts momentarily forgotten as she read his poem.

"When life feels heavy, and hope fades to gray,
Remember, I am here, just a heartbeat away.
Though worlds may lie between us, and doubts may rise above,
I'll hold the space between us with my unwavering love."

Leila's fingers hovered over the keys, a small, reluctant smile tugging at her lips. He always knew what to say, always seemed to have the words she needed, even when she couldn't ask for them. She typed out a response, hesitating before sending it.

LeilaWrites: Thank you, David. You always know just what to say. But... sometimes I wonder if this is all real. If we're just two people searching for something we can't find. It's hard for me to believe that... that something this beautiful could be true.

There was a pause as she waited for his reply, the seconds stretching into what felt like an eternity. She felt exposed, vulnerable, her words carrying pieces of her heart she wasn't sure she was ready to share.

DavidEvergreen: Leila, I understand. It's natural to feel that way, especially with everything you've been through. I can't make the doubts disappear, but I want you to know that I'm here, as long as you need me to be. We don't have to have all the answers right now. Sometimes, it's enough to just be here, together.

She closed her eyes, feeling the warmth of his words wash over her. His patience was a balm, soothing the insecurities that had taken root in her heart. But the fear remained, lurking beneath the surface, a reminder of the walls she had built around herself, walls she wasn't sure she was ready to let go of.

She took a deep breath, her mind drifting back to memories she rarely allowed herself to revisit. Moments from her past flickered in her mind—a childhood filled with uncertainty, relationships that had left her feeling hollow, a marriage that had turned into a quiet kind of loneliness. She had spent so long keeping these memories locked away, tucked behind carefully constructed walls that even she rarely dared to cross.

But with David, those walls felt fragile, thin enough to break if she allowed herself to be vulnerable. The thought terrified her, but it also made her wonder if, maybe, she was ready to share these parts of herself. She typed slowly, her words coming together one by one, each one carrying the weight of her past.

LeilaWrites: David, can I tell you something? It's hard for me to believe in... well, in anything lasting. I grew up feeling like love was something temporary, something you couldn't trust. My parents... they weren't bad people, but they were distant, always caught up in their own lives. And then, as I got older, I kept finding myself in relationships where I felt invisible, like I was just a placeholder. It's why I ended up here, in this marriage that feels more like an arrangement than anything else. Sometimes I wonder if I'm capable of being truly loved.

She stared at the message, her heart racing as she hit send. The silence that followed was thick, her mind filling with a thousand thoughts, a thousand fears. What would he think? Had she said too much? But before she could let her doubts spiral, his reply appeared, each word like a gentle hand reaching through the darkness.

DavidEvergreen: *Leila, thank you for sharing that with me. I can't imagine how hard that must have been. But I want you to know that you are not invisible to me. You're not a placeholder. You're real, you're here, and I see you. I don't know what the future holds, but I know that right now, in this moment, you are important to me. And I'll be here, for as long as you'll have me.*

Her hands trembled as she read his words, a strange mix of relief and vulnerability washing over her. She felt the weight of his presence, a quiet reassurance that wrapped around her like a warm blanket. He didn't push, didn't pry—he simply let her be, offering his support without expectation.

They continued talking, their conversation weaving through memories and unspoken fears. She shared pieces of her past, small fragments that she had kept hidden for so long. And in return, David shared his own experiences, the quiet struggles he had faced, the pain he had learned to live with. There was a rawness to their exchange, an honesty that felt like peeling back layers they had both kept hidden, even from themselves.

The hours slipped by, the outside world fading as they opened up to each other, their words filling the spaces they had once kept guarded. David's understanding, his unwavering patience, was a balm to the parts of herself that had long felt fractured and unseen. She felt the beginnings of something new, a small, tentative hope that perhaps, despite the distance and the doubts, they had found something worth holding on to.

As the night wore on, David sent her another poem, this one softer, gentler, a reflection of the quiet strength he offered her.

"Love is not a promise, nor a guarantee,
It is the gentle faith that, together, we'll see."
"Though fear may cloud, and doubts may grow,

I'll stand by you, through highs and lows."

Leila read the poem, her heart swelling with a mixture of gratitude and longing. She wanted to believe in his words, wanted to hold on to the hope he offered her. But a part of her still held back, clinging to the familiar safety of her doubts.

LeilaWrites: David, thank you. I don't know how you do it, how you always know the right thing to say. I still don't have all the answers, but... maybe I'm starting to believe that there's something worth waiting for.

His reply was simple, yet it held a weight that wrapped around her like a promise.

DavidEvergreen: Take all the time you need, Leila. I'm not going anywhere.

As she lay in bed that night, his words echoed in her mind, a steady rhythm that lulled her into a quiet peace. She didn't have all the answers, and the doubts were still there, but she felt a glimmer of hope, a tentative belief that perhaps, just perhaps, they could find a way through the darkness together.

And as sleep claimed her, she held on to his words, letting them fill the empty spaces in her heart, a quiet promise of something beautiful and real.

Chapter 6: Crisis Point

Leila sat in the silence of her small apartment, her thoughts tangled in a web of frustration, sadness, and exhaustion. The weight of her marriage felt like a suffocating shroud, pressing down on her until she could barely breathe. Every day seemed to blend into the next, a string of half-hearted conversations, stifling routines, and unspoken resentments. She couldn't remember the last time she felt joy in her own home; even the simplest moments had become a struggle to endure. She tried to numb herself to the pain, tried to go through the motions, but the exhaustion was catching up with her, draining her of any remaining strength.

It wasn't that her husband was a bad man; he was kind enough, reliable in the ways that mattered. But kindness alone wasn't enough to fill the growing chasm between them. She had tried to talk to him, to explain the emptiness she felt, but he didn't seem to understand. Or perhaps he just didn't want to. Every attempt at honesty had been met with silence, a wall of indifference that left her feeling even more isolated.

Her mind wandered to David, his steady presence a quiet balm in the storm of her life. He had been her confidant, her friend, her anchor in a world that felt increasingly unstable. His words had become a refuge, a place she could go to when the walls of her life seemed too close. But even as she found solace in their connection, she knew it was a lifeline that couldn't last forever. The reality of her marriage, her responsibilities, the fear of stepping into the unknown—all of it held her back, a chain she couldn't bring herself to break.

The sound of her phone vibrating broke the silence, and she glanced down to see a message from David.

DavidEvergreen: *Leila, I know you're going through so much, and I wish I could be there to make it easier. I don't have all the answers, but I want you to know that I believe in you. You're stronger than you know. Take things one day at a time. You'll find your way through.*

Leila closed her eyes, letting the words settle over her like a blanket. His faith in her was unwavering, a steady force that reminded her of the possibility of hope, even in the darkest moments. But as much as she wanted to believe him, her doubts lingered, clinging to her like shadows.

She typed out a response, her fingers trembling slightly.

LeilaWrites: *Thank you, David. I wish I could believe in myself the way you believe in me. Everything feels so heavy, and I don't know how to move forward. Sometimes I feel like I'm trapped, like there's no way out.*

The seconds ticked by in silence before his reply appeared.

DavidEvergreen: *Leila, I know it's hard to see beyond the pain, but there's always a way. Sometimes it's just a matter of letting go, trusting that the path will appear when you're ready. And remember, you're not alone. I'm here, no matter what.*

Leila exhaled slowly, feeling a surge of gratitude mingling with her fear. His words were like a lifeline, tethering her to the possibility of a life beyond her current reality. But as comforting

PATIENCE OF THE HEART

as his support was, she knew she couldn't rely on it forever. She would have to face her fears, make a decision about her future—a decision that would either free her or break her completely.

The days that followed were a blur of tension and quiet arguments, each one leaving her feeling more drained, more uncertain. She found herself pulling away, retreating into herself, and each time her husband asked what was wrong, she found herself at a loss for words. How could she explain the emptiness, the quiet ache that seemed to fill every corner of her life?

One evening, after yet another strained conversation, she found herself staring at the blank page of her journal, her pen poised above the paper, but the words refusing to come. It was as if her voice had been silenced, her emotions too tangled to put into words. In desperation, she reached for her phone, opening her messages with David.

LeilaWrites: I feel like I'm drowning, David. I don't know how much longer I can keep pretending. But the thought of leaving... it terrifies me. What if I make the wrong choice? What if I end up alone, with nothing to hold on to?

She hit send, her heart pounding as she waited for his reply. Part of her feared he would grow tired of her doubts, her endless cycle of fear and uncertainty. But, as always, his response came swiftly, filled with the quiet reassurance she had come to depend on.

DavidEvergreen: Leila, I understand the fear. Change is terrifying, especially when you're stepping into the unknown. But sometimes, staying where you are is even scarier. You deserve a life that brings you joy, not just survival. Trust yourself. Trust that you have the strength to find your way.

Her eyes filled with tears as she read his words, a wave of emotion washing over her. He was right. She couldn't keep living like this, trapped in a life that no longer felt like her own. But the path forward was still unclear, shrouded in shadows that made her hesitate. She knew she needed to take a step, to make a choice, but fear held her back, a relentless force that refused to let go.

Days passed, each one a quiet struggle between her desire for freedom and the fear of what lay beyond. And then, one evening, she received an unexpected message from an unfamiliar number.

Hello, Leila. My name is Rachel. I'm a friend of David's, and he shared some of your poetry with me. I'm in publishing, and I wanted to let you know that I think your work is beautiful. If you're interested, I'd love to discuss the possibility of publishing some of your pieces.

Leila's heart skipped a beat, her fingers trembling as she read the message. She had shared bits of her poetry with David, small fragments of her soul she had kept hidden from everyone else. But she hadn't expected him to share them with anyone, hadn't imagined that her words could hold any value beyond the quiet solace they brought her.

Her thoughts raced, a mix of excitement and fear swirling within her. She wanted to believe that this was real, that her words could have meaning, but doubt clouded her mind. She hesitated, wondering if she was ready to take this step, to put herself out into the world in a way she had never done before.

After a few moments, she typed out a response, her heart pounding with a mixture of hope and trepidation.

Thank you, Rachel. I'm honored that you think my work is worth publishing. I'd love to learn more about the process and what it would entail.

The reply came quickly, Rachel's words filled with encouragement and enthusiasm.

Rachel: Leila, I truly believe your voice deserves to be heard. We can start small, perhaps with a collection of your poems. You'll have full control over what you share. Take your time, and know that I'm here to support you every step of the way.

Leila's eyes filled with tears, a quiet gratitude filling her heart as she realized that, maybe, this was the beginning of something new. She hadn't dared to dream of a future where her words, her voice, could matter. But now, with David's support and the opportunity that Rachel had offered, she felt a glimmer of possibility, a fragile hope that perhaps she could create a life beyond the shadows of her past.

As she lay in bed that night, her mind drifted back to David's words, the quiet faith he had shown in her from the very beginning. She knew the path ahead would be difficult, filled with uncertainty and fear, but for the first time, she felt ready to face it. She wasn't alone. She had David, she had her own voice, and maybe, just maybe, she had the strength to find her way forward.

Chapter 7: Dreams of What Could Be

Leila lay on her bed, eyes fixed on the ceiling as her thoughts drifted to David. She had never allowed herself to think this way before, to entertain the idea of a life beyond the narrow confines of her marriage. Yet, in the quiet of the night, when everything felt still, she found herself imagining what it would be like to be with him, to share more than just words on a screen.

It had started as a small flicker, a fleeting thought she had quickly dismissed. But now, that flicker had grown into a steady glow, warming her heart with a hope she had almost forgotten she could feel. She could picture it so clearly—the way his eyes might light up when they finally saw each other, the way his voice might sound, deeper and richer than she could imagine through text. It was these moments, these small glimpses of a possible future, that kept her going.

The quiet chime of her phone brought her back to the present. She reached over, smiling as she saw his name lighting up her screen. He had messaged her, just as she had been thinking of him.

DavidEvergreen: Leila, I know this sounds silly, but I can't stop thinking about what it would be like to meet you, to actually sit across from you and talk. I wonder what it would feel like to be near you, to hear you laugh in real time, not just in my imagination.

She felt her heart skip, a strange mix of excitement and fear flooding her chest. It was the first time he had spoken so openly about meeting, and while the thought thrilled her, it also made her aware of the weight she was carrying, the shadows of her past and the restraints of her present.

Her fingers hesitated over the keyboard before she typed back, her words carefully chosen.

LeilaWrites: *I've been thinking about it too, more than I'd like to admit. Sometimes it feels like you're already here, like you're sitting beside me, talking me through the hardest days. But... there's still so much standing in the way. My life, my marriage. I don't know if I'm strong enough to break free from it all.*

The seconds ticked by, her message hanging in the space between them. She felt exposed, vulnerable, her heart laid bare in a way she hadn't expected. But David's reply came swiftly, his words filled with the quiet reassurance she had come to depend on.

DavidEvergreen: *Leila, I understand. I don't want you to feel pressured, not for a second. Whatever happens, whatever you decide, I'm here. I believe that sometimes, life has a way of bringing us where we're meant to be, even if it takes longer than we'd like.*

She felt her chest tighten, a tear slipping down her cheek as she read his words. He never pushed, never demanded more than she could give. He simply waited, patiently holding space for her as she tried to find her way through the fog of her life. And in that patience, she found the strength to hope, to dream of a life that felt like her own.

In the days that followed, their conversations grew deeper, their words weaving a tapestry of dreams and possibilities. They spoke of quiet moments, of laughter shared over coffee, of long walks and late-night conversations. She let herself imagine it, let herself believe in the beauty of a future unburdened by the pain of her past. For the first time in years, she felt the faint stirrings of freedom, a life unencumbered by the weight of her marriage.

Yet, even as she dreamed, the reality of her life lingered like a shadow, pulling her back with its reminders of duty and responsibility. Her husband, once a distant figure in the background, had begun to notice her absence, the way she seemed to drift further away with each passing day. Their conversations had grown shorter, filled with an uncomfortable silence that seemed to stretch on endlessly. She knew he could sense the change in her, the way she no longer fit neatly into the life they had built.

Her chronic pain, too, had become a constant companion, a reminder of the limitations she couldn't escape. There were days when it flared so intensely that she could barely get out of bed, let alone imagine a future that required strength and resilience. But each time she found herself sinking, each time the pain seemed too much to bear, David was there, his words a gentle balm that soothed her wounded spirit.

One evening, after a particularly painful day, she messaged him, her vulnerability laid bare in her words.

LeilaWrites: David, I don't know if I can do this. Some days, the pain is so overwhelming that I can't imagine a life beyond it. I'm scared. Scared that this is all I'll ever know, that I'll be trapped in this cycle of pain and emptiness forever.

His reply came almost immediately, as if he had been waiting for her, sensing her need for comfort.

DavidEvergreen: Leila, I can't pretend to know what you're going through, but I know that you're stronger than you realize. Pain doesn't define you. It's a part of your story, but it's not the whole story. You have so much beauty, so much light within you. I see it every time we talk, every time you share a piece of your heart with me.

She closed her eyes, letting his words wash over her, a quiet reassurance that filled the empty spaces within her. It wasn't a solution, wasn't a cure for the pain, but it was enough to remind her that she wasn't alone, that there was someone who saw her, who believed in her, even on the days when she struggled to believe in herself.

As the weeks passed, their conversations became a lifeline, a bridge that connected them across the miles and the barriers of their separate lives. They shared their dreams, their fears, the quiet moments of hope and doubt that colored their days. And with each message, each whispered promise of a future, Leila felt herself inching closer to the possibility of something new, something real.

One night, as they spoke of their dreams, David sent her a message that left her breathless, his words a gentle reminder of everything she had come to cherish about him.

DavidEvergreen: Leila, I know that life is complicated, and I know that we're both carrying so much. But I want you to know that, whatever happens, you're not alone. I'll be here, whether it's tomorrow, or a year from now, or even longer. I'll wait, because I believe in us, in this connection we've built. I believe that one day, we'll find a way to bridge the distance.

Her heart ached as she read his words, a mix of joy and sorrow flooding her chest. She wanted to believe in his promise, wanted to hold on to the hope he offered her. But fear lingered, the weight of her life pressing down on her, reminding her of the realities she couldn't escape.

And yet, even in the midst of that fear, she found herself daring to dream. She imagined a life where pain didn't hold her captive, where love wasn't something to be endured but something to be cherished, shared openly without fear. She imagined a world where David was more than just words on a screen, where he was a presence in her life, a hand to hold, a shoulder to lean on.

It was a fragile hope, a tentative belief that reality could one day align with their dreams. But it was there, a glimmer of light in the darkness, a quiet promise that perhaps, despite everything, happiness was within reach.

As she lay in bed that night, her thoughts filled with the dreams they had shared, she felt a peace settle over her, a soft whisper of possibility that filled her heart. She didn't know what the future held, didn't know if their dreams would ever become reality, but for the first time, she was willing to believe in the beauty of what could be.

Chapter 8: The First Attempt

Leila woke with a sense of anticipation she hadn't felt in years. Today was the day—after months of late-night conversations, whispered dreams, and tentative hopes, she and David were finally going to meet. She could barely believe it, the idea of seeing him face-to-face felt almost surreal, like a dream she was afraid to wake from. For once, her heart was light, her mind free from the usual cloud of doubt and uncertainty.

She stood in front of the mirror, a nervous excitement fluttering in her stomach as she brushed her hair, straightening the loose strands. It wasn't a special day, yet it felt monumental, a turning point in her life that had taken so long to reach. She glanced at her phone, checking for any updates from David, her heart racing as she imagined what it would be like to finally see him, to hear his voice in real time, to bridge the distance that had kept them apart for so long.

Her phone buzzed, and she quickly reached for it, her excitement momentarily dimmed by an unexpected message from work. She opened it, her brow furrowing as she read the text from her supervisor.

Supervisor: Leila, we have an urgent project that needs immediate attention. I know this is last minute, but is there any way you can come in today?

Her heart sank, a wave of frustration flooding her chest. She had already taken the day off, cleared her schedule so she could focus on her meeting with David. But her job wasn't exactly understanding when it came to personal time. She thought about ignoring the message, pushing her phone aside, but the sense of obligation pulled at her. She couldn't afford to risk her position, not with her circumstances.

With a sigh, she typed out a response, trying to explain that she had prior commitments. But the reply came swiftly, her supervisor insisting that it was urgent, that there was no one else available. Leila glanced at the time, calculating how long it would take to finish the work and whether she could still make it to her meeting with David. Her excitement dimmed, a gnawing sense of dread settling in her stomach as she realized that this might derail everything.

Taking a deep breath, she decided she would go in, work as quickly as she could, and leave the second she was finished. It was the only way. She couldn't let this ruin the day she had been looking forward to for so long.

Hours later, Leila found herself still at work, her frustration mounting as the clock ticked forward. The project was more complex than she'd anticipated, each task piling onto the next, consuming more time than she had planned. Her mind kept drifting to David, to the plans they had made, and the thought of disappointing him filled her with a guilt she couldn't shake.

Finally, after what felt like an eternity, she finished the last task, quickly gathering her things as she rushed out the door. She checked her phone, her heart sinking as she saw the time. She was late, far later than she had expected, and she knew that David would be waiting, wondering what had happened. Her chest tightened as a familiar ache began to creep into her limbs, her chronic pain flaring from the stress of the day.

She sent him a quick message, her hands trembling as she typed.

LeilaWrites: *David, I'm so sorry. Work kept me longer than expected. I'm on my way now, but I don't know if I'll make it in time. Please don't be mad.*

The reply came quickly, his words filled with the same patience and understanding he had always shown her.

DavidEvergreen: *Leila, it's okay. I understand. I'm just glad you're safe. We can always reschedule if it's too much for you. I don't want you to push yourself if you're not feeling well.*

She closed her eyes, feeling the weight of his words settle over her. Even in her disappointment, his kindness was a balm, a reminder that he cared for her well-being above all else. But the thought of rescheduling, of pushing this moment further away, felt unbearable. She wanted to see him, needed to see him, to bridge the gap that had kept them apart for so long.

Determined, she continued on her way, fighting through the pain that pulsed in her joints, a constant reminder of the toll her life had taken on her. She arrived at the small café where they had planned to meet, her heart racing as she scanned the room, searching for him.

But he wasn't there.

Panic flared in her chest as she checked her phone, scrolling through their messages to see if she had missed an update. Then she saw it—a message he had sent an hour ago, one she hadn't seen in her rush.

DavidEvergreen: *Leila, something's come up on my end. My car broke down on the way, and I'm stuck waiting for a tow truck.*

I'm so sorry. I was looking forward to this more than you know. Let me know if you're okay, and we'll figure this out.

Leila's heart sank, a wave of disappointment washing over her as she realized that their plans had been thwarted, not just by her circumstances but by his as well. It felt like the universe was playing a cruel joke, teasing them with the possibility of closeness only to pull it away at the last moment. She sat down at a small table, her body heavy with fatigue, her heart aching with the weight of missed chances.

She typed out a reply, her fingers trembling with a mix of sadness and frustration.

LeilaWrites: David, I'm so sorry. I wish things had gone differently. It's like the universe is keeping us apart, no matter how hard we try.

His response was immediate, his words filled with the same steady hope he had always shown her.

DavidEvergreen: Leila, maybe it just wasn't the right time. I believe that when it's meant to happen, nothing will stand in our way. We'll try again, and we'll keep trying until we get it right. Don't lose hope.

She closed her eyes, letting his words wash over her, a quiet comfort in the midst of her disappointment. She could feel the tension in her body easing, her pain softening as she allowed herself to believe, just for a moment, that he was right—that maybe, this wasn't the end, but just a small detour on the path they were meant to take together.

The café buzzed with life around her, the hum of voices and the clinking of cups a gentle reminder that the world continued to turn, even as her dreams seemed to hang in the balance. She took a deep breath, her heart heavy yet filled with a quiet determination. She wouldn't let this setback keep her from believing, from hoping. David was still there, still waiting, just as he had always been, his faith in their connection unwavering.

In the days that followed, they returned to their usual rhythm, their conversations a steady balm that soothed the ache of missed chances. David continued to share his poetry, his words filled with the quiet reassurance that had become her anchor. One evening, he sent her a new poem, a reflection of the hope they both held onto, even in the face of disappointment.

"Love doesn't vanish in the space of a missed day,
It lingers, it waits, finding its own way.
Through the setbacks, the tears, and the pain we endure,
It holds, it strengthens, steady and pure."

Leila read the poem, her heart swelling with a mix of gratitude and longing. She knew that their path wouldn't be easy, that there would be more obstacles, more delays. But David's words, his quiet strength, reminded her that their connection was worth fighting for, worth the patience and the perseverance it demanded.

And so, she held on, her hope a fragile but resilient thing, a promise to herself that, one day, they would find a way to be together, no matter how long it took.

Chapter 9: Holding On Through the Storm

The days stretched into weeks, and each passing day felt like a new test of Leila's patience and faith. The anticipation she had carried for their meeting had dulled, replaced by a quiet ache that lingered in her chest. She tried to keep busy, to fill her days with work and routine, but nothing seemed to ease the emptiness that had taken root. She longed to see David, to feel his presence in a way that went beyond their messages and late-night calls.

She found herself pulling back, her doubts creeping in like shadows. What if they never met? What if this connection, as beautiful as it was, was destined to remain confined to screens and words? It was a thought she tried to push away, but it lingered, gnawing at her hope, making her question everything they had built together.

One night, as she lay in bed, staring up at the ceiling, she felt the weight of her fears pressing down on her. She reached for her phone, scrolling through their old messages, reading over his words, each one a reminder of the love and faith he had poured into their connection. But tonight, even his words felt distant, a reminder of how far apart they truly were.

Unable to shake the feeling, she typed out a message, her heart heavy as she admitted the thoughts she had been trying to bury.

LeilaWrites: David, I don't know if I can keep doing this. Some days, it feels like I'm holding onto something that isn't real, like I'm clinging to a dream that will never come true.

The seconds ticked by, her message hanging in the air, and she wondered if he would understand, if he would see through the words to the fear that lay beneath them. His response came quickly, filled with the quiet strength she had come to depend on.

DavidEvergreen: Leila, I know this is hard. I feel it too, every day. But I believe in us. I believe that, one day, we'll find a way to be together. It may not be easy, and it may not be soon, but I have faith that it will happen. Don't lose hope.

She felt a tear slip down her cheek, his words a balm to her wounded heart. She wanted to believe him, wanted to hold onto the faith he had, but the doubts were relentless, a constant reminder of the miles and circumstances that kept them apart. She typed back, her fingers trembling as she tried to put her feelings into words.

LeilaWrites: I wish I had your faith, David. I wish I could see the future as clearly as you do. But sometimes, it just feels like we're fighting against something we can't control.

There was a pause, a silence that stretched between them, before his reply appeared.

DavidEvergreen: Leila, it's okay to feel that way. I don't expect you to have all the answers, and I don't expect you to feel the same way I do. All I ask is that you keep an open heart, that you let yourself believe in the possibility of us, even if it's just a small, quiet hope. I'll be here, however long it takes.

His words lingered in her mind, a steady presence that anchored her, even as her doubts swirled around her. She didn't know how he did it, how he managed to hold onto his faith with such unwavering certainty. But in that moment, she felt a glimmer of his strength, a small spark that reminded her of the beauty they had found in each other, even across the distance.

The days continued to pass, each one filled with moments of hope and doubt, a constant push and pull that left her feeling drained. She tried to focus on the positives, on the quiet joys they shared through their messages, the poems he sent her, each one a reflection of the love and patience he held for her. But there were days when the distance felt insurmountable, when the reality of their situation weighed heavily on her, threatening to pull her under.

One evening, after a particularly difficult day, she received a message from David that felt like a lifeline, a reminder of the connection they shared.

DavidEvergreen: *Leila, I wrote something for you today. I hope it brings you a little light, even on the darkest days.*

Below his message was a new poem, each line carefully written, a piece of his heart offered up to her.

"*Love endures the quiet ache, the space that lies between,*
It waits, it breathes, in spaces still unseen.
Though miles and time may keep us far,
Our hearts remain where our bodies are."

She read the poem slowly, letting each word sink in, feeling the quiet reassurance that radiated from his words. It was as if he had reached across the distance, his hand steadying hers, reminding her that they were still connected, still bound by the love they had found in each other. Her doubts softened, the ache in her heart easing as she allowed herself to believe, just for a moment, that they would find a way through this.

As the weeks went on, she found herself leaning on him more, his unwavering faith a constant reminder that love could endure, even in the face of distance and time. They spoke of their dreams, of the life they hoped to build together, each conversation a small act of defiance against the odds that stood in their way. And with each message, each whispered promise, she felt her heart begin to open, her hope slowly growing stronger, a quiet resilience that reminded her of the beauty they had found together.

Yet, even as she clung to his faith, the reality of her life loomed large, a shadow that refused to let go. Her chronic pain had begun to flare more frequently, the stress of their situation taking its toll on her body. There were days when the pain was so intense that she could barely move, her limbs heavy with exhaustion, her mind clouded with the weight of her struggles. But each time she felt herself sinking, each time the pain seemed too much to bear, David was there, his words a balm that soothed her wounded spirit.

One night, as she lay in bed, her body aching, she sent him a message, her vulnerability laid bare in her words.

LeilaWrites: David, I don't know how you do it. How you manage to hold onto hope, even when everything feels so uncertain. Some days, it feels like I'm fighting a losing battle, like this pain will never end, like we'll never find a way to be together.

His reply came swiftly, his words filled with the same quiet strength she had come to cherish.

DavidEvergreen: Leila, you don't have to be strong all the time. It's okay to feel scared, to feel like you're losing hope. But remember, you're not alone. I'm here, and I believe in you, in us. Together, we'll find a way, even if it takes longer than we'd like.

She closed her eyes, letting his words wash over her, a quiet comfort that eased the ache in her heart. She knew that their path wouldn't be easy, that there would be more obstacles, more delays. But his faith, his unwavering belief in their connection, was a reminder that love could endure, even in the face of doubt and fear.

As the night wore on, they continued to talk, their words weaving a tapestry of hope and resilience. David shared his dreams, his visions of a future where they could finally be together, and with each word, he breathed life into the fragile hope that had taken root in her heart. She didn't know what the future held, didn't know if they would ever find a way to bridge the distance, but for the first time, she felt a glimmer of peace, a quiet assurance that, no matter what happened, their love would endure.

And as she drifted off to sleep, her heart filled with a quiet determination, she held onto his words, a steady presence that anchored her in the storm, a reminder that sometimes, love was worth the wait.

Chapter 10: Breaking Free

Leila sat on the edge of her bed, her heart racing as she stared at the papers in her hand. The words "Petition for Divorce" stared back at her, a stark reminder of the decision she had made, the step she was finally ready to take. For so long, her life had felt like a maze of dead ends, each path leading her back to the same hollow existence. But now, with the papers in her grasp, she felt the first stirrings of something she hadn't felt in years: freedom.

It had taken months to reach this point, to find the strength to break free from a life that had become little more than a shadow of who she was. David's presence had been the guiding light through it all, his words a gentle reminder that she deserved happiness, that she was capable of creating a life that felt like her own. She had doubted herself, questioned her worth, but his quiet faith had been unwavering, a steady anchor that held her through every storm.

With a deep breath, she set the papers down, her gaze drifting to the open laptop on her desk. Her inbox was filled with responses from publishers, all interested in her poetry. She had started small, sharing her work through online platforms, hesitantly submitting a few poems to literary journals. But to her surprise, the response had been overwhelmingly positive. Editors had praised her unique voice, her raw honesty, and offers for publication had begun to trickle in, each one a small victory that fueled her determination to keep going.

One evening, she had shared the news with David, her excitement tempered by a lingering fear that her success was fleeting. But he had been thrilled, his words filled with the same unwavering support he had shown her from the very beginning.

DavidEvergreen: *Leila, this is only the beginning. You have so much to offer the world, and I'm so proud of you for taking this step. Keep going. Don't let anything hold you back.*

His words had filled her with a quiet confidence, a belief that maybe, just maybe, she was capable of building a life that felt like her own. She had started to envision it, piece by piece—a new job, a place of her own, a life where her happiness was no longer dependent on the approval of others. It was a dream she had once believed was out of reach, but now, with each step forward, it felt more real, more attainable.

The sound of her phone buzzing pulled her from her thoughts, and she glanced down to see a message from David. She smiled, her heart swelling with gratitude as she opened it.

DavidEvergreen: *Leila, I was thinking of you today. I wrote something that I think speaks to where you are right now. I hope it brings you strength.*

His poem appeared beneath the message, each line carefully crafted, a reflection of the journey she had been on.

"In breaking free, she found her wings,
No longer bound by silent strings.
She rose above the weight of fear,
Her heart alive, her path made clear."

She read the poem slowly, letting each word sink in, feeling the quiet strength that radiated from his words. It was as if he had seen into her heart, understood the battles she had fought, the courage it had taken to reach this point. With a deep breath, she typed out a reply, her fingers trembling as she shared a piece of her own heart with him.

LeilaWrites: *David, thank you. You have no idea how much your words mean to me. I've spent so long feeling trapped, convinced that I wasn't strong enough to change my life. But you've helped me see that I am capable, that I can create something beautiful, something real. I don't know where this path will lead, but I know that I'm finally ready to find out.*

His response was immediate, his words filled with the same steady faith that had carried her through the darkest moments.

DavidEvergreen: *Leila, you've always had that strength within you. I've just been lucky enough to witness it. This is your time, your chance to build the life you deserve. I'm here, every step of the way.*

With a renewed sense of determination, she closed her phone, her gaze drifting to the stack of job listings on her desk. She had spent weeks researching, carefully selecting positions that aligned with her skills, roles that promised a fresh start, a chance to rebuild her life on her own terms. Her heart pounded as she looked over the list, each one a symbol of the life she was beginning to create.

In the days that followed, she threw herself into her job search, her efforts rewarded with a promising interview at a local publishing company. The position was entry-level, but it offered the stability she needed, the chance to be part of a world she had once only dreamed of. The interview had gone well, and as she left the building, her heart felt lighter than it had in years, a quiet hope blossoming within her.

A few days later, the call came—a formal job offer, a new beginning. She accepted with a joy she hadn't felt in years, her mind racing with the possibilities that lay ahead. She would have her own income, a chance to support herself, to build a life free from the constraints of her past. She shared the news with David, his response filled with the same boundless enthusiasm he had always shown her.

DavidEvergreen: *Leila, this is incredible! I knew you could do it. You're building something beautiful, something that belongs to you. I can't wait to see where this journey takes you.*

As she settled into her new job, her days filled with purpose and a sense of fulfillment she had never known, she took the next step in her journey. She filed for divorce, the paperwork a tangible reminder of the life she was leaving behind, a life that no longer held her captive. It wasn't easy—there were moments of doubt, flashes of fear that threatened to pull her back. But each time she faltered, she reminded herself of the strength she had found, the resilience that had carried her through every challenge.

She found a small apartment downtown, a modest space that felt like her own. It was quiet, filled with light, a blank canvas that she could shape into a home. She filled it with books, plants, small touches of color that brought her joy. She set up a small writing nook by the window, a place where she could let her creativity flow, where her thoughts and dreams could find a home on the page.

And as she settled into her new life, she continued to write, her poetry a reflection of the journey she had been on, the transformation she had undergone. With David's encouragement, she began to compile her poems into a collection, each piece a testament to her strength, her resilience. She submitted her manuscript to a few publishers, and to her surprise, several expressed interest, each one offering her the chance to share her words with the world.

One evening, as she sat by her window, watching the city lights twinkle in the distance, she received a message from her publisher—a formal acceptance of her poetry collection, with plans for publication in the coming months. She felt a surge of pride, a quiet joy that filled her heart as she realized that she was finally living the life she had always dreamed of.

Her phone buzzed with a new message, and she smiled as she saw David's name.

DavidEvergreen: *Leila, I'm so proud of you. You've come so far, and you've built something truly beautiful. This is only the beginning. Keep going, keep dreaming. You have so much to offer the world.*

She closed her eyes, his words a gentle reminder of the journey they had shared, the bond they had forged. She didn't know what the future held, but for the first time, she felt ready to face it, her heart filled with hope, her path clear.

And as she sat there, her heart brimming with gratitude, she realized that she was no longer waiting for life to happen. She was living it, fully and unapologetically, a quiet force of resilience and strength. She had broken free, and in doing so, she had found herself.

Chapter 11: The Long-Awaited Meeting

The months that followed felt like a slow but steady climb toward a life Leila had once thought impossible. Her new job brought a sense of purpose she hadn't felt in years, her days filled with projects that sparked her creativity, coworkers who shared her passion for words. She had her own space now, a small, cozy apartment that she'd filled with warmth and light. There were still moments when doubts crept in, nights when the silence of her newfound independence was louder than she had expected, but each day she felt stronger, more rooted in her own life.

Her poetry had also begun to take on a life of its own. What had started as a quiet side project had blossomed into a modest success. Her collection had been published, and while she wasn't making a fortune, the sales were steady enough to provide a bit of extra income. She would see her book displayed on the shelves of a local bookstore, tucked between collections by poets she had long admired, and it filled her with a quiet pride. It was her voice, her story, reaching people in ways she had never imagined. And in the background of it all, David was there, his steady presence a constant source of encouragement and warmth.

Their conversations continued, each message a thread that wove them closer, even across the miles. They shared the small details of their days, the moments of joy and frustration, the quiet dreams that had become part of their shared story. But as the months passed, the desire to finally see each other in person grew stronger, an unspoken yearning that lingered in every exchange. They had tried before, only to be thwarted by circumstances, but this time felt different. They had both come so far, each of them building a life that felt true, and it was finally time to bring their worlds together.

One evening, after a particularly long day at work, Leila sat down with her phone, her fingers trembling slightly as she typed out the question that had been on her mind.

LeilaWrites: *David, I think I'm ready. I think it's time for us to meet. What do you think?*

His reply came quickly, his excitement palpable even through the screen.

DavidEvergreen: *Leila, I've been waiting for this moment. Tell me when and where, and I'll be there.*

They spent the next few days making plans, each detail discussed with a sense of care and anticipation. They decided to meet halfway, at a quiet café in a town that held no memories for either of them, a neutral space where they could finally bring their connection into the physical world. Leila felt a mix of excitement and nerves, the reality of their meeting settling over her like a quiet storm. She had imagined this moment countless times, had dreamed of what it would feel like to finally see him, to hear his voice, to share space with him. But now that it was real, her mind filled with questions, a swirl of anticipation and uncertainty.

The day of their meeting arrived, and she found herself standing in front of the mirror, smoothing her hair, her heart pounding with a mixture of joy and fear. She wore a simple dress, something comfortable yet elegant, her makeup subtle, her jewelry minimal. She wanted to feel like herself, to bring her true self into this moment they had both waited so long for.

The café was a small, cozy space with a quiet charm, nestled on a corner surrounded by trees that cast dappled sunlight through the windows. She arrived a few minutes early, her heart racing as she found a small table by the window, her eyes scanning the room as she waited. The anticipation was electric, each moment stretching into eternity as she glanced at the door, waiting for him to appear.

And then, he was there. She saw him before he saw her, his figure framed by the doorway as he scanned the room, his expression a mix of hope and nerves. Her breath caught in her throat, her heart skipping as she took him in—the familiar warmth in his eyes, the quiet strength in his posture, the kindness that radiated from him. He looked exactly as she had imagined, yet somehow more real, more present, more hers.

He spotted her, a slow smile spreading across his face as their eyes met. She felt a rush of emotions, a wave of relief and joy washing over her as he made his way toward her. When he reached the table, they simply stood there for a moment, taking each other in, the weight of the moment settling around them. No words were spoken, but none were needed; everything they had shared, everything they had waited for, was there, in the silence between them.

Finally, David broke the silence, his voice soft yet steady.

"Leila," he said, his tone filled with warmth and awe, as if he were seeing her for the first time and yet had known her all along. "It's... it's so good to finally see you."

She smiled, her own voice trembling slightly as she replied. "David... I can't believe we're really here."

They sat down, a comfortable silence settling between them as they each took a moment to gather their thoughts. It was surreal, the feeling of being in the same space, of seeing each other beyond the confines of a screen. They ordered coffee, their conversation slow at first, each of them savoring the reality of the moment. But as they spoke, the familiar rhythm of their connection returned, their words flowing easily, each laugh, each shared glance a reminder of the bond they had built.

At one point, David reached across the table, his hand finding hers, a simple gesture that spoke volumes. She felt a warmth radiate from his touch, a grounding presence that reminded her of everything they had shared, everything they had overcome to reach this point. His thumb brushed lightly over her fingers, a small, tender motion that sent a thrill through her, the weight of their journey held in that single touch.

They talked for hours, their conversation winding through stories, shared memories, dreams for the future. He told her about the quiet moments of his days, the small things that reminded him of her, the way he had counted down the days until they could meet. She shared her own journey, the struggles she had faced, the strength she had found in his words. It was as if they were catching up on a lifetime of moments, each story a piece of the puzzle that had brought them together.

As the sun began to set, casting a warm glow through the windows, David pulled a small notebook from his bag, his gaze soft as he handed it to her.

"I've been writing something," he said, a hint of shyness in his voice. "It's... well, it's for you."

She took the notebook, her fingers brushing over the worn cover as she opened it to the first page. There, in his careful handwriting, was a poem, each line a reflection of the journey they had been on, the love they had found in each other.

"In the quiet spaces, love took root,
A tender bloom in a world of strife.
Through words and distance, fears and doubt,
We found each other, and we found our life."

Her heart swelled as she read, her eyes blurring with tears as she looked up at him, her voice barely a whisper. "David, it's beautiful. Thank you."

They sat there in the quiet, the intensity of the moment settling over them. She wanted to say so much more, to tell him how much he meant to her, how his words had changed her life. But in that moment, all she could do was reach for his hand, her fingers intertwining with his as they sat together, their hearts open, their future unwritten.

As they left the café, walking side by side under the soft glow of the streetlights, Leila felt a peace she had never known, a quiet certainty that, no matter what lay ahead, they had found something real, something worth holding onto. There was still so much they didn't know, so many questions left unanswered, but in that moment, none of it mattered.

Together, they had created a world that was theirs, a place where love was possible, even in the face of doubt and fear. And as they walked into the night, their laughter filling the air, she knew that this was only the beginning, a journey that would continue, a love that would endure.

Chapter 12: A New Beginning

The months that followed were a tapestry of moments Leila had once only dreamed of, each day filled with the quiet magic of discovering life with David by her side. It was as if the universe had finally aligned, their paths converging in a way that felt effortless, almost predestined. She moved through her days with a lightness she had never known, her chronic pain almost entirely receding, the weight of her past dissolving like morning mist under the warmth of his presence.

Their mornings often began with laughter, David bringing her coffee as they sat by the window, their voices filling the space with stories, dreams, and small intimacies that painted their life in colors she hadn't dared to imagine. The days were simple, yet each one held a sense of wonder, as if every moment was a gift they had waited years to open. She would catch herself smiling at nothing in particular, her heart filled with a peace she had never thought possible.

One evening, as twilight cast a soft glow over their living room, they settled onto the couch, his arm draped around her shoulders as she leaned into him, savoring the warmth of his presence. The world outside seemed to fade away, the hum of the city replaced by the steady rhythm of his breathing, the quiet strength of his love. She looked up at him, her voice soft as she whispered, "David, do you ever think... this is almost like a dream?"

He chuckled, brushing a strand of hair from her face. "Sometimes. But if it is, it's the best dream I've ever had."

Their eyes met, and in that moment, the space between them seemed to shrink. She felt the air shift, charged with anticipation, her heartbeat quickening as his gaze softened, tracing her face as if memorizing every line. Slowly, he leaned in, his lips brushing hers in a tender, hesitant kiss. It was soft at first, a gentle exploration that spoke of patience and longing, but as she responded, it deepened into something more—a kiss that carried the weight of every unspoken word, every moment they had spent waiting for this.

Leila felt a warmth spread through her, a fire that chased away the last remnants of doubt and fear. His hands moved to her waist, pulling her closer, their bodies fitting together as if they had always belonged that way. The kiss was both grounding and electric, a silent promise exchanged in the quiet of their embrace. When they finally pulled back, her breath came in soft, uneven waves, her eyes searching his, finding the same awe mirrored in his gaze.

"Leila," he whispered, his voice husky with emotion, "I never thought I could feel this way. You make everything else fade away."

She smiled, resting her forehead against his, their breaths mingling as they held each other, the silence speaking louder than any words. In that moment, she felt the full force of their journey—every message, every poem, every night spent yearning for this closeness. It was real, tangible, and hers.

In the weeks that followed, they found a rhythm that felt as natural as breathing. Her chronic pain, once a constant shadow in her life, had almost entirely faded, her body and mind buoyed by the peace she had found in his presence. She continued to write, her poetry more vibrant, more alive than ever, each word a reflection of the love and joy that now colored her world.

They spoke of the future with a gentle optimism, their plans woven together with dreams and hopes, each conversation a step toward the life they were creating. She marveled at the ease with which they communicated, each of them attuned to the other's thoughts, their silences as meaningful as their words. David became her anchor, her safe haven, a presence that filled the empty spaces in her life with a warmth she had never known.

On one particularly peaceful night, as the city lights sparkled in the distance, David handed her a small notebook, his gaze soft as he watched her open it. Inside was a collection of his poems, each line carefully written, a reflection of their journey, of the love they had found together.

Her breath caught as she read, her heart swelling with a quiet awe as she took in the words.

"In your eyes, I found the stars,
In your voice, a gentle balm.
Together, we healed the broken parts,
Our hearts entwined in quiet calm."
"Through every trial, we found our way,
A steady light in darkest night.
Now, hand in hand, we greet the day,
Our love, a flame of endless light."

Tears blurred her vision as she looked up at him, her voice trembling with emotion. "David... thank you. You've changed my life in ways I can't even begin to describe."

He smiled, reaching for her hand, his touch a steadying presence. "Leila, you don't have to thank me. Loving you has been the greatest gift of my life."

They sat together in the quiet warmth of the evening, the city lights casting a soft glow over the room as they shared a moment of unspoken understanding. It was as if everything they had been through, every struggle, every triumph, had led them here, to this place of peace and love.

As they spent more time together, Leila found herself reflecting on the journey they had shared, the quiet strength that had carried them through. She no longer felt haunted by the past, her fears replaced by a gentle confidence, a belief in herself that she had once thought impossible. With David by her side, she felt capable of anything, her heart open to the endless possibilities of the life they were building.

One night, as they lay together, her head resting on his chest, she felt a surge of gratitude, a quiet joy that filled her heart as she whispered, "I never thought I'd find this... find you."

He held her close, his voice a soft murmur as he replied, "Leila, you were worth the wait."

Their first embrace had been tentative, filled with the weight of years of yearning, but with each day, their closeness grew more natural, more vital. Sometimes, she would catch him watching her, his eyes filled with a warmth that made her heart flutter, and she would smile, knowing that her presence was as much a comfort to him as his was to her. They would share quiet mornings tangled in sheets, conversations whispered between kisses, the world beyond their walls forgotten.

Each night, as they shared soft words and laughter, David would pull her into his arms, pressing a kiss to her temple, and she would feel the rush of love swell within her. It was a love that had defied distance, doubt, and time, and now it was hers to hold, as real as the beating of her heart.

In that moment, she knew that, no matter what the future held, they would face it together, their love a steady flame that would carry them through whatever lay ahead.

And as she drifted off to sleep, held in his embrace, she knew that their story was just beginning, a journey that would continue to unfold, each chapter a testament to the strength of their bond, the beauty of their love.

Don't miss out!

Visit the website below and you can sign up to receive emails whenever Teri Dourmashkin publishes a new book. There's no charge and no obligation.

https://books2read.com/r/B-A-QHNBB-HNEEF

BOOKS2READ

Connecting independent readers to independent writers.

Did you love *Patience of the Heart*? Then you should read *A Veil of Dreams*[1] by Teri Dourmashkin!

A Veil of Dreams: Echoes of the Unseen is a collection of deeply personal and evocative poems that explore the intricate dance between the seen and the unseen, the physical and the spiritual, the painful and the healing. With each verse, Dr. Teri Dourmashkin invites readers on a journey of self-discovery and emotional reflection, revealing the resilience of the human spirit. This anthology delves into the realms of love, loss, inner strength, and the quest for meaning amidst life's most challenging moments. Through her poetic lens, Dourmashkin

---

1. https://books2read.com/u/mgwAp6

2. https://books2read.com/u/mgwAp6

offers a tapestry of words that resonate with anyone who has ever sought to find light in the darkness, peace in chaos, and love in the depths of the soul. Whether you are on a path of healing, seeking inspiration, or simply looking to connect with the profound emotions that make us human, A Veil of Dreams serves as both a companion and a guide through the complexities of the heart and soul.

Read more at terilove.com.

Also by Teri Dourmashkin

Ripples of Serenity
Waves of Enlightenment
Elixir of Love
Love's Eternal Dance
Skyward Ballet
Beneath the Surface
Lighthouse of Dreams
A Veil of Dreams
Patience of the Heart

Watch for more at terilove.com.

About the Author

Dr. Teri Dourmashkin, Ed.D., is the founder of a minimalist skincare line, known for its natural ingredients and handcrafted batches. Alongside her skincare expertise, she is a passionate poet, blending beauty and wellness in both her professional and creative pursuits.terilove.com

Read more at terilove.com.

Milton Keynes UK
Ingram Content Group UK Ltd.
UKHW030853111124
451035UK00001B/86